SUNDAY PANCAKES

Maya Tatsukawa

Dial Books
for Young Readers

FOR SHOKO & KARIN

Dial Books for Young Readers
An imprint of Penguin Random House LLC, New York

First published in the United States of America by Dial Books for Young Readers, an imprint of Penguin Random House LLC, 2022

Copyright © 2022 by Maya Tatsukawa

Penguin supports copyright. Copyright fuels creativity, encourages diverse voices,
promotes free speech, and creates a vibrant culture. Thank you for buying an authorized edition of this book and for
complying with copyright laws by not reproducing, scanning, or distributing any part of it in any form without permission.
You are supporting writers and allowing Penguin to continue to publish books for every reader.

Dial & colophon are registered trademarks of Penguin Random House LLC.

Visit us online at penguinrandomhouse.com.

Library of Congress Cataloging-in-Publication Data is available.

Manufactured in Spain • ISBN 9780593406632 • EST • 10 9 8 7 6 5 4 3 2 1

Design by Mina Chung • Text set in Mikado and handlettered by Maya Tatsukawa

The art was created with stencils, handmade textures, and photoshop.

The publisher does not have any control over and does not assume any responsibility for author or third-party websites or their content.

TODAY IS SUNDAY, WHICH MEANS...

PANCAKES
FOR BREAKFAST!

IT'S REALLY SIMPLE— JUST THESE INGREDIENTS.

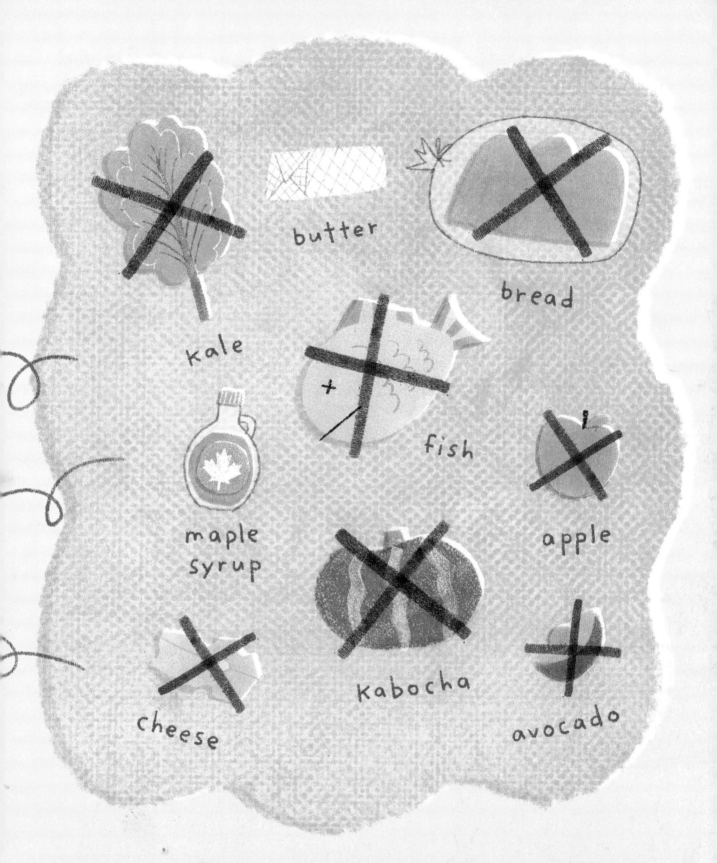

MAYBE MY FRIENDS HAVE SOME.

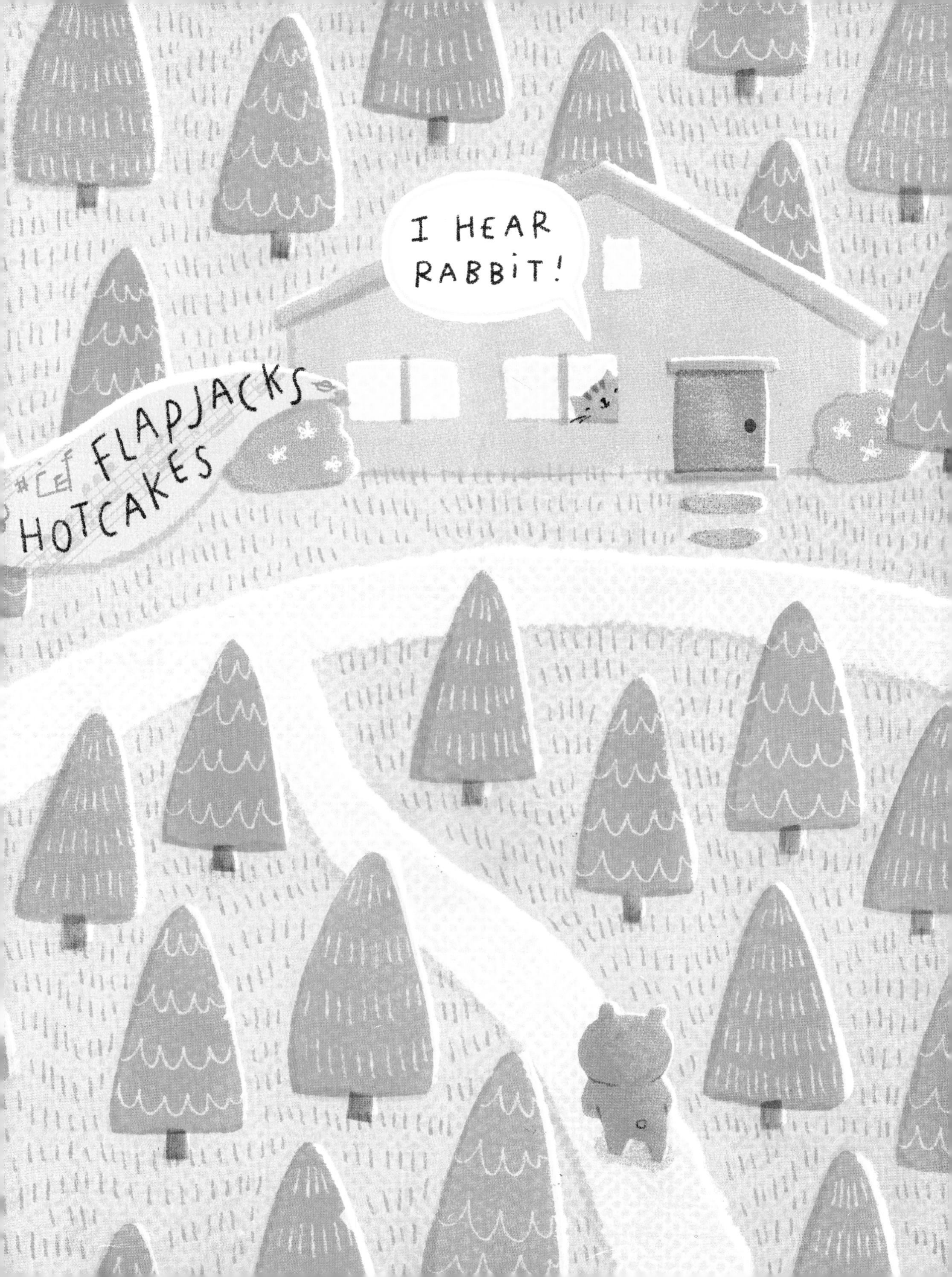
I HEAR RABBIT!
FLAPJACKS
HOTCAKES

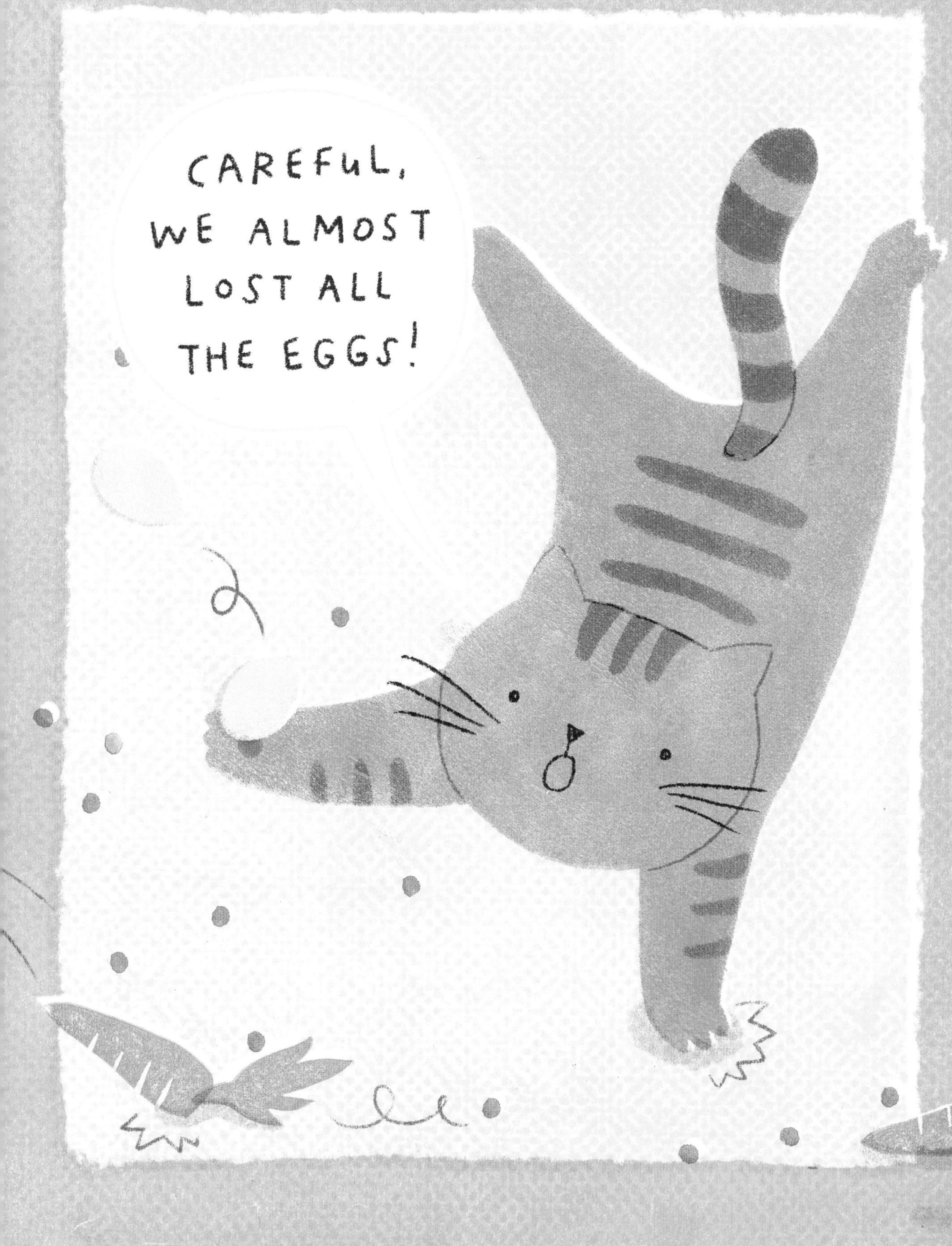
CAREFUL, WE ALMOST LOST ALL THE EGGS!

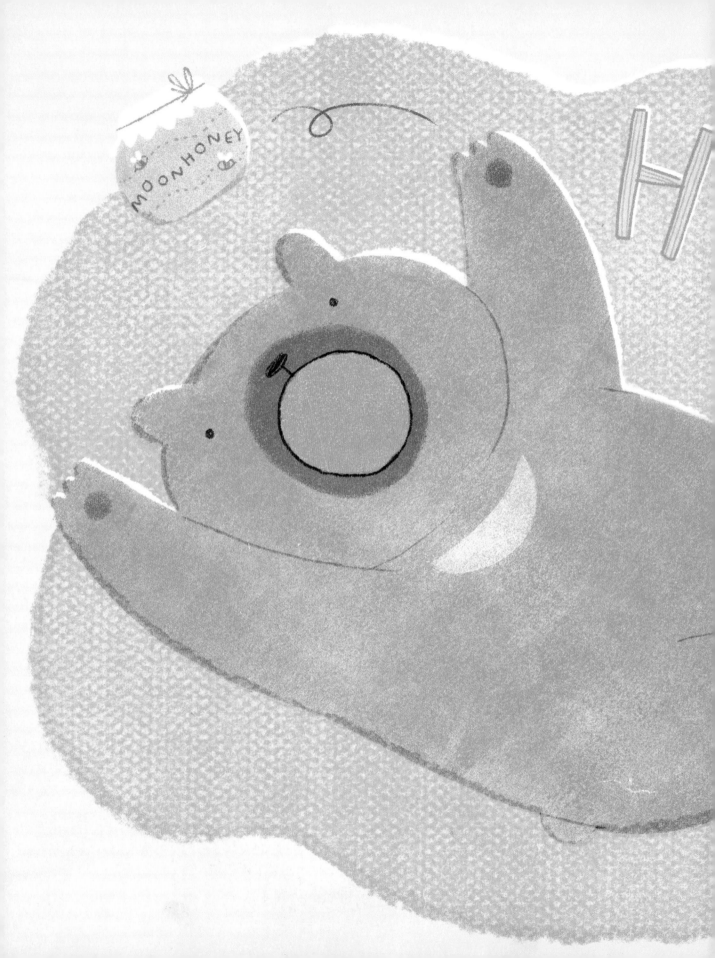

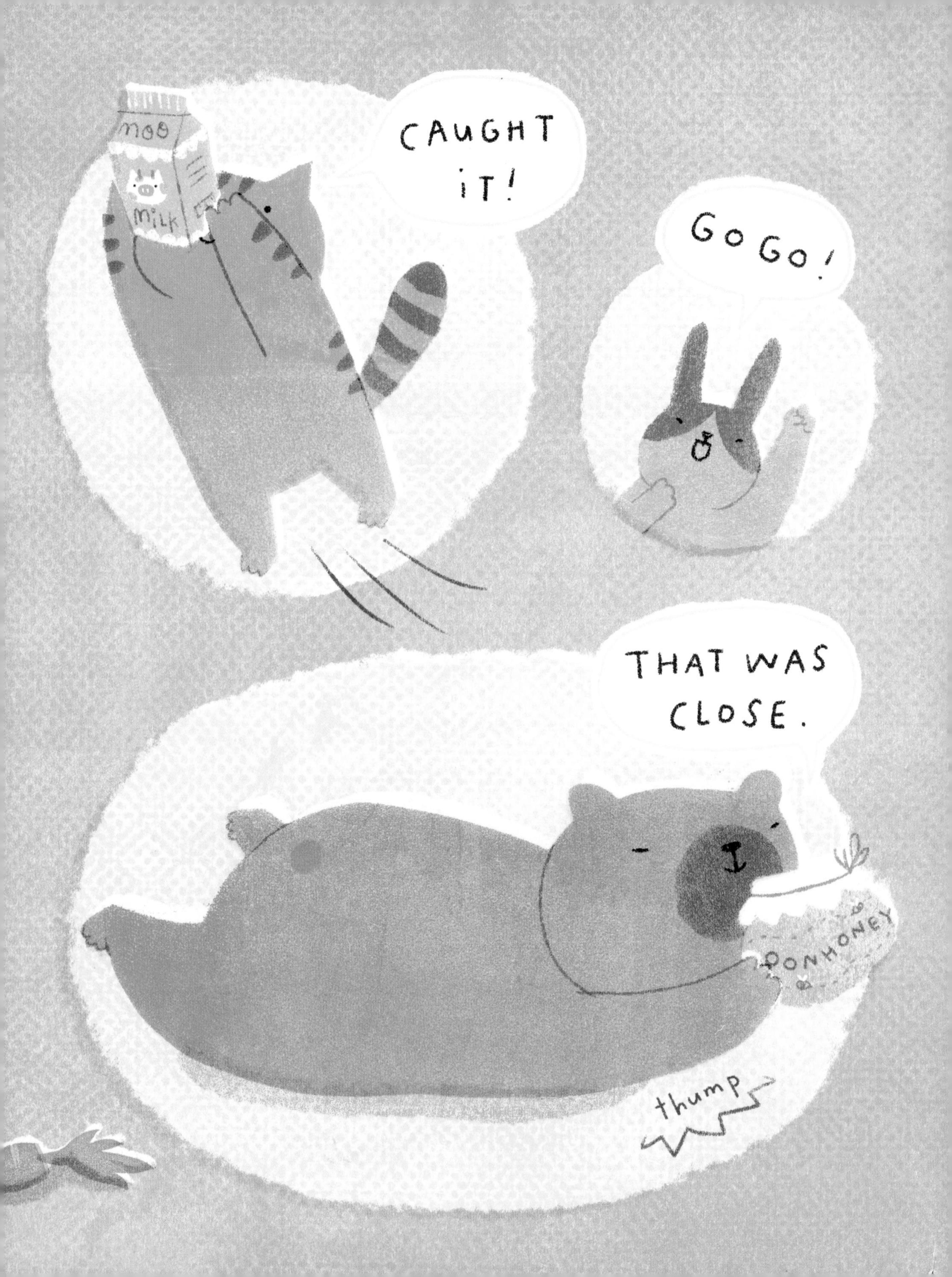
moo
milk
CAUGHT IT!
GO GO!
THAT WAS CLOSE.
thump

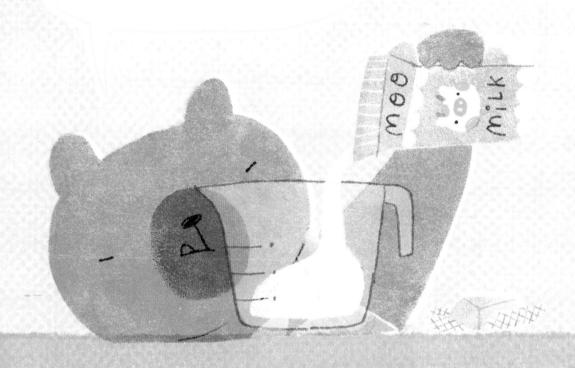

OH !
I'LL POUR
THE FLOUR.

WHAT
SHOULD
I DO?

PO

MOONBEAR TURNED INTO A POLAR BEAR!
haha
haha
haha
Baking Powder
SUGAR

AND NOW IT'S TIME TO COOK!

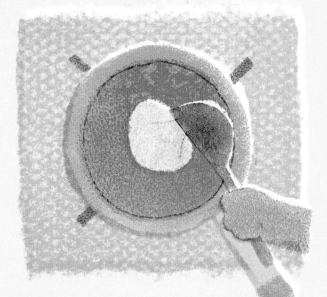

FIRST, POUR
THE BATTER.

THEN, ONCE
BUBBLES FORM,

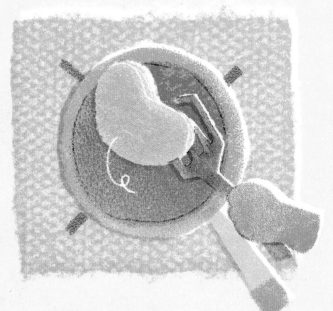

IT'S READY
TO FLIP!

COOK THE
OTHER SIDE AND...

FLIP

flip

flip

flip

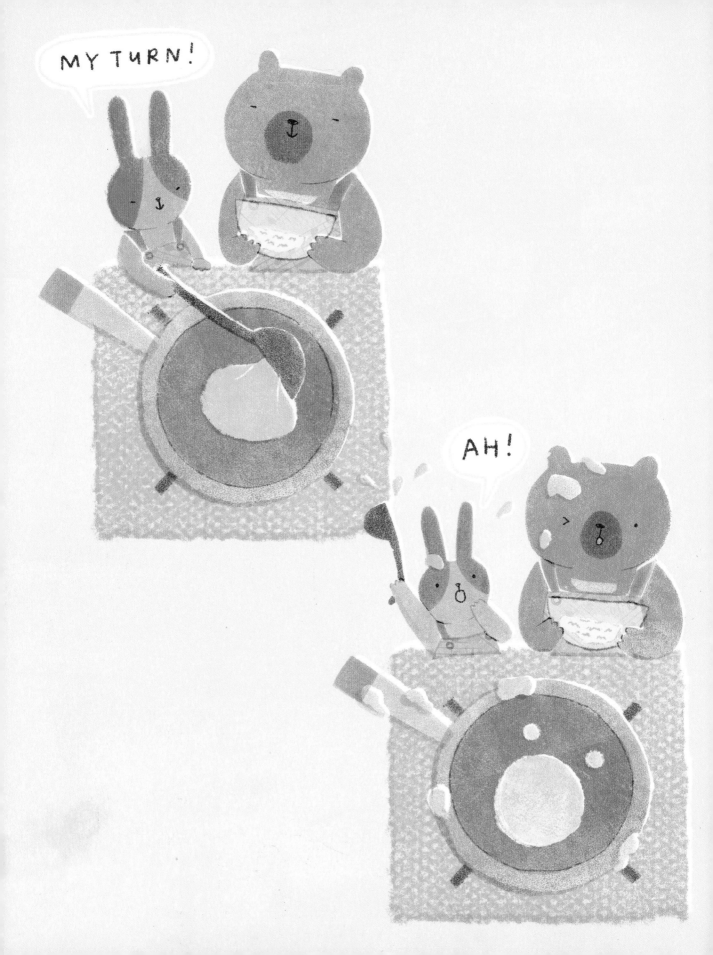

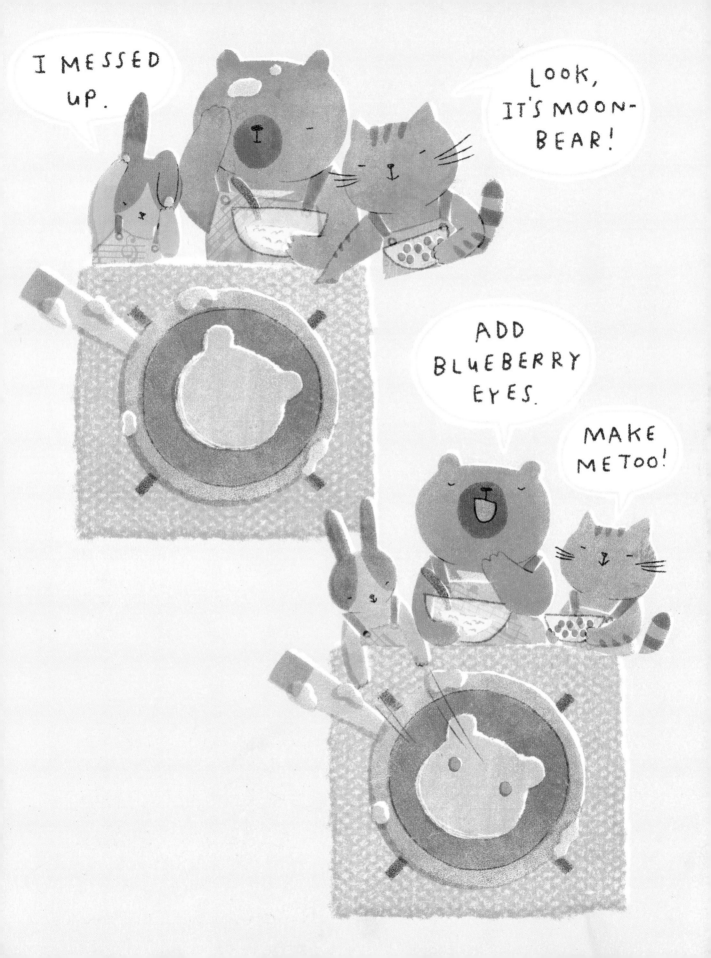

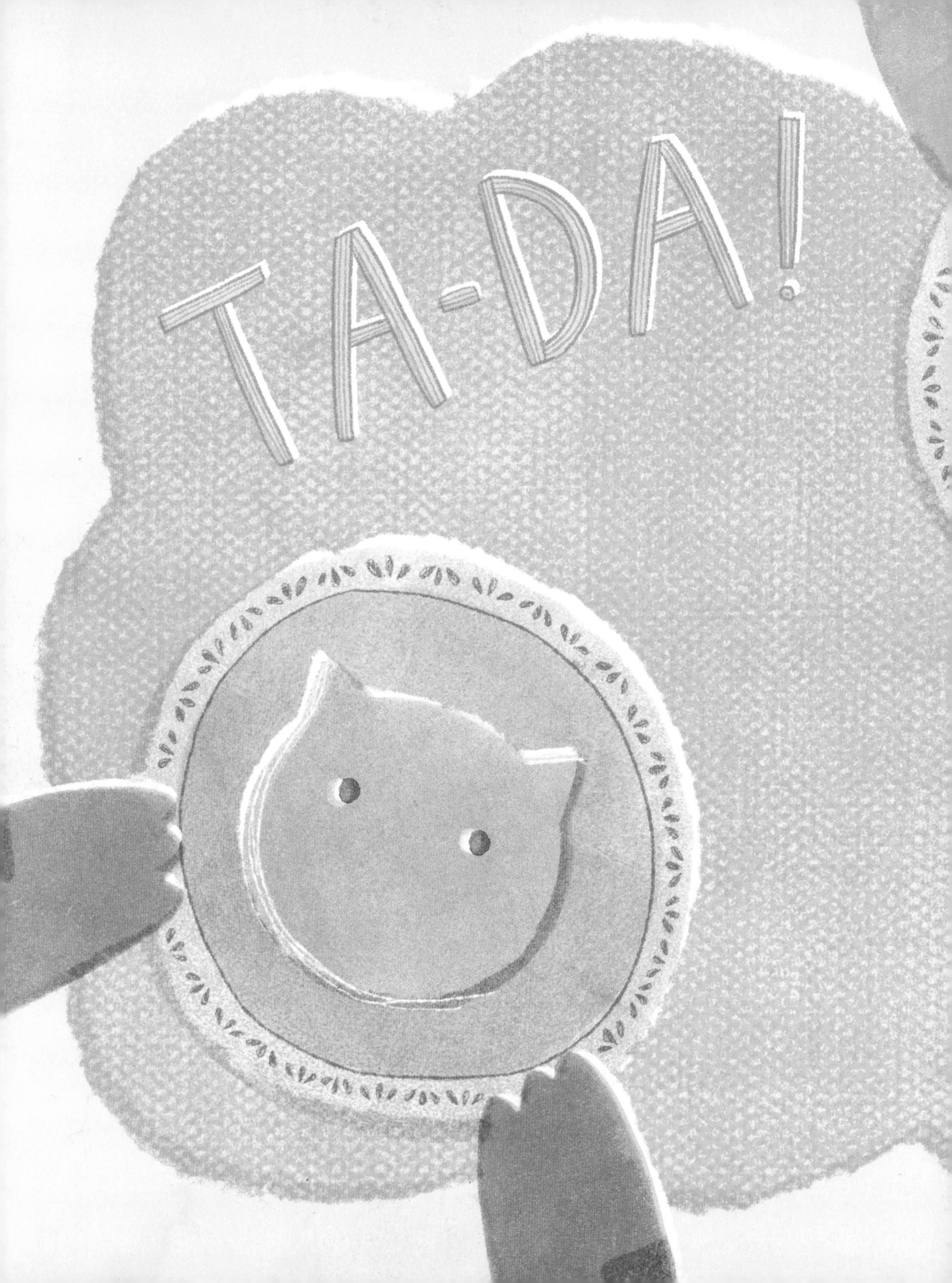
TA-DA!

IT'S US!

LET'S EAT!

...is PANCAKES FOR DINNER!

CAT'S SUNDAY PANCAKES

(MAKES ABOUT 15 MINI PANCAKES OR 5 BIG ONES)

INGREDIENTS

DRY (BOWL A)	WET (BOWL B)
1⅓ CUP FLOUR*	1¼ CUP MILK
3 tsp BAKING POWDER	3 tbsp BUTTER
3 tbsp SUGAR	1 EGG
½ tsp SALT	

*FOR GLUTEN FREE, REPLACE 1:1 WITH A GF BLEND FLOUR.